A Middle Eastern No

A Middle Eastern No

Jill Widner

SOUTHWORDeditions

First published in 2019
by Southword Editions
The Munster Literature Centre
Frank O'Connor House, 84 Douglas Street
Cork, Ireland

Set in Adobe Caslon 12pt

ISBN 978-1-905002-68-9

Contents

Acknowledgements

The three stories included in *A Middle Eastern No* are part of a collection in progress set in Iran and Saudi Arabia, where my father worked as a petroleum engineer throughout the 1970s.

"When Stars Fell Like Salt before the Revolution" is based partly on a road trip I took with my mother from Ahvaz to Isfahan and Shiraz in 1974 when I was nineteen and she was fifty-two. It was selected by Douglas Glover as one of two short fiction honorable mentions in *The Fiddlehead's* 23rd annual short fiction contest (University of New Brunswick, Canada), and published in Issue 259 in spring 2014. In October 2014 it was selected by Clifford Garstang to be included in the inaugural issue of *Everywhere Stories: Short Fiction from a Small Planet* (Press 53). It was also selected by Joyce Russell as one of nine highly commended stories in the 2013 Seán O'Faoláin International Short Story Competition.

"Yalda & Zhila" is a work of fiction inspired in part by "The Turban, Defiled by Suicide Bombers, Has Biblical and Emotional Roots," an op-ed published in The *New York Times* by Farzaneh Milani, chairwoman of the Department of Middle Eastern and South Asian Languages and Cultures at the University of Virginia. It was published in the May/June 2019 issue of *Kenyon Review Online*.

"Alice in Abqaiq" is set in Saudi Arabia where I taught briefly at what was then called the Dhahran International School.

My gratitude to my husband, Phil Gallagher; my family; my friends from all corners of the world and all periods of my life; my colleagues, my students, the president, the administration, and the board of trustees of Yakima Valley College, who have supported my efforts for the last 26 years, in spite of my idiosyncrasies, as someone who teaches writing from the point of view of a writer who writes.

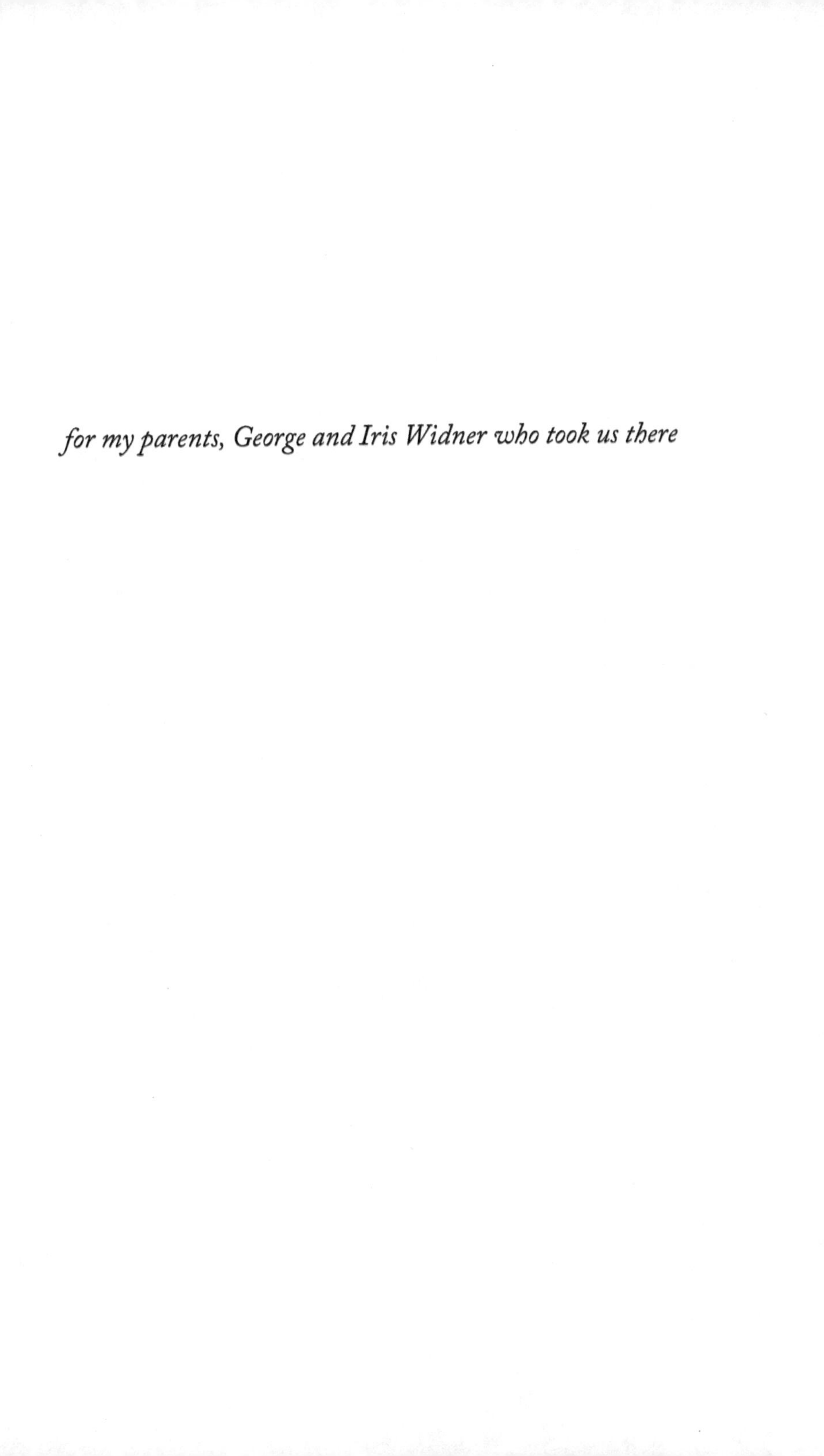

for my parents, George and Iris Widner who took us there

WHEN STARS FELL LIKE SALT
BEFORE THE REVOLUTION

Sylvie stands at the window, wrapped in a blanket, the dawn in the distance, brightening the dusting of snow that has fallen overnight in the courtyard below. The dun-colored grass is frozen. The stone fountain and concrete pools, empty and scattered with leaves.

The second-floor rooms on the other side of the courtyard are larger than the room Sylvie shares with her mother. They have balconies, each with a private ceiling, a mosaic of tile in a vaulted arch that is the same turquoise blue as the dome-shaped roof of the mosque, visible through the branches of the trees. At the top of the dome, a weathervane, like an axe-head in the shape of a crescent, gleams in the sun like a coin.

And then there is no mosque. No rose hips dangling from bare branches. A girl is lifting her hand. She's smiling at Sylvie and, turning it over, she touches the mound at the base of her fingers, where the skin is marked with crosshatched lines like ideographs she can't read, and the girl won't tell her what they say.

There is movement behind the railing of the balcony on the other side of the courtyard. The curtains part. A man stands at the window in loose, dark, pajama-like clothing. His hair hangs over his forehead. He brushes it back and raises his gaze to her window, where she stands bare-legged in a loose t-shirt. Their eyes meet. Or they don't. She isn't sure. The curtains close.

When Sylvie awakens she finds a note on her mother's bed, instructing her to meet her downstairs in the Caravanserai Room where tea is served. She opens the curtains and stares through the glass. There are the pools, scattered with leaves. There is the mosque through the trees. She turns her hands over. There are the cross-hatchings like number signs etched in the skin.

Sylvie finds her mother seated on a mound of cushions facing
a low table, eating dry toast and drinking hot tea with lemon
in a china cup. Sylvie tells the waiter she would like her tea the
Iranian way and studies her palms while she waits. He brings a
gold-rimmed vessel the size of a shot glass on a saucer scattered
with transparent shingles of crystalized sugar. The waiter shakes
his head no when Sylvie starts to break a piece into the glass. He
motions for her to put it in her mouth. "There it will dissolve," he
tells her. "This is the Irani way."

Sylvie's mother wants to shop for Kilim. They wander beneath
the vaulted ceilings of the bazaar, a maze of brick lanes crowded
with kiosks, searching for the carpet merchants. Sometimes they
find themselves at the dead end of a narrow alley, sometimes
back where they started beneath the open arches that face
Shahrdari Square.

In a fabric stall, a shopkeeper unfurls a bolt of bright cloth
and drapes it over the partition that divides his stall from another.
Plain-colored chadors, blue, black, or grey, hang on coat racks and
translucent headscarves, like slips made of insect wings swing from
wooden screens.

In a spice stall, mountains of saffron are piled beside mountains
of rice. Cardamom and cumin, like ground, colored chalk are
spread on silver trays. Beside these, baskets of dried lime, apricots,
figs and dates. At the doorway, waist-high burlap bags folded back
at the top contain dried lentils and beans and something black and
dried that looks like a kind of mushroom.

At the front of another stall, a man is arranging pomegranates
in tiers on a wooden cart. He splits one in half, peels back the
membrane, and spills the bright red arils into Sylvie's open hand.

Sylvie likes to bargain and finds that she's good at it. In a
metal shop, she barters for a round box with a man whose skin is
blackened with copper dust.

"That is not enough," he says, when Sylvie offers a price. "You
see," he says, prying the box apart with his fingers. "This box has a
lid. And here, is an inscription."

"But the lid is too tight," Sylvie counters. "And look at your fingers. This box is very dirty."

He takes the box out of her hands and rubs it with a cloth he has pulled from his pocket. "This box can be clean."

He is handsome, Sylvie thinks. Many Irani men are handsome. Even the old men. The goldsmith in the jewelry shop is such a man. He introduces himself as Sahar Jazin and asks Sylvie's mother if she and her daughter would like to watch him work. Sylvie's mother is reluctant, but follows Sylvie and the bearded man in the white turban, the loose trousers, and the long white shirt through a beaded curtain.

At the back of the room Sahar Jazin sits on a wooden stool that faces a workbench. He opens one of many drawers in a cupboard built into the wall and, with a pair of fine-tipped pincers, rummages among what sound like bits of gravel. He drops a shard of gold the size of a fishing weight into a mortar beneath which a small fire is smoldering.

"What shall I make for you?" Sahar Jazin asks.

Sylvie points to the turquoise ring on his little finger. Except for what looks like a moon-shaped Persian letter worn into the shank, it is plain. "A ring like yours."

"This ring is from the holy city of Mashad. It is very old. I have many rings much more beautiful than this inside the case." He leads the way back through the curtain to the front of the shop and points to the jewelry on display, but Sylvie shakes her head no.

Sahar Jazin unlocks one of the drawers behind the counter and holds a gold loop, decked with bits of turquoise against her nostril. "How do you like this?"

Sylvie laughs. "But I would need two. For my ears."

"Of course." He nips a fine length of gold in two with a pair of wire clippers, and then, with a pair of pincers, coils one piece around the other until he has twisted it closed in a knot. He opens a different drawer and slides flat squares of macled turquoise smaller than the tip of a match onto the open end of the curved wire and motions for Sylvie to turn her head to the side. "Take the other one away," he says, and when she has, slips the open end of the loop through the hole in the lobe of her ear.

He hands Sylvie the other ring. "Put this one on the other side."

Sylvie pushes her hair behind her ear and tries, but it won't go in. "I need a mirror. I can't see."

"No mirror. You must feel with your fingers." She tries again.

"You do it," she says at last.

When the earring is in place, Sahar Jazin asks Sylvie's mother if he may know her daughter's name. He removes a fountain pen from another of the drawers and writes something on a sheet of graph paper he tears from a small spiral notebook. He takes his time, and Sylvie watches the Persian script appear beneath his fingers, a net of filigree, the ink like watercolor before it dries on the paper.

Sylvie watches closely as Sahar Jazin writes something more. "You must keep this," he says when he is finished.

Sahar holds the curtain aside for Sylvie's mother to pass through. The beads brush the floor and for a brief moment he is alone in the room where Sylvie is studying what he has written on the small piece of paper.

"What I have written is for you. Not for anyone else. Do you understand?"

Sylvie doesn't, but nods and follows him to the counter at the front of the shop, where her mother is opening her wallet. When they have agreed on a price, Sahar Jazin escorts them to the door. "Khoda hafez," he says, more to Sylvie than to her mother. He holds the back of his hand against his chest, then turns it over and holds his palm for a moment over his heart.

At the end of the lane are the Persian carpet stalls. The bright, geometric patterns of the Kilim Sylvie's mother has been searching for are everywhere, unfurled on tables, stacked in rolls, pulled open on the dusty stone floor. But Sylvie has grown tired of bartering and tells her mother that she will meet her back at the hotel.

"It's an easy walk. Twenty minutes at most from the square. If you find a carpet you like, say you want it delivered to the hotel. You know what they say. She travels fastest who travels alone."

"What?"

"Rudyard Kipling."

The middle of Shahrdari Square is a rose garden, but because it is January, the branches, like the branches of the rose bushes in the courtyard of the hotel, are bare except for the tips of the stems, which are weighted down with the red-brown husks of the hips. Sylvie wants one for a souvenir.

She is tucking the rose hip into the inside pocket of her parka, looking both ways to cross the busy Karim Khan e Zand Boulevard, thinking of all of the things Shiraz is known for—Shiraz, the city of poetry; Shiraz, the city of nightingales and moonlight; Shiraz, the house of learning, when a white dog with swollen teats runs in front of her, nipping at the heels of a man pedaling past on a bicycle. A girl in tall, rubber boots and a knee-length dress runs after the dog into the middle of the street. The top of her head is wrapped in a red scarf; beneath it, her hair hangs long down her back. The dog turns around when she calls and, wriggling, follows her back to the sidewalk.

Sylvie crouches to pet the dog and looks at the girl. Her eyes are like the turquoise in Sahar Jazin's ring, both rough like stone and shining, but green not blue. The girl touches the dog's head and slips her hair behind her ear. To show off her earring, Sylvie thinks, then sees that what she had thought was a silver feather is a grey knotted string.

"Eight puppies she has. Come. I will show you."

Sylvie hesitates but, curious, she follows the girl and the white dog back inside the bazaar, except now they are at the opposite end of the cross-shaped structure. They walk beneath the vaulted brick ceiling, turning down one lane and then another until they come to a path that slopes underground and ends at a den, a kind of crawl-space beneath the building, but tall enough to stand. In a corner, a handful of children surround a pile of lumber. Beneath the boards, on a piece of flattened cardboard, a swarm of squirming puppies is huddled together in a pack, their eyes still shut. The mother dog lies down and, squealing softly, the puppies begin to suckle. Sylvie watches them, nestled against the mother dog's abdomen, which is when she remembers reading in her mother's guidebook that, in Farsi, the root of Shiraz, *shir*, generally means lion, but it can also mean milk.

And then a man is approaching. The girl says something to the man in Farsi, and in English he tells Sylvie she can take the white one for twenty rials.

Less than thirty cents. Sylvie wants to say yes, but she lowers her eyes and shakes her head no. "Their eyes aren't even open. Anyway, tomorrow we fly back to Ahvaz, and, the week after that, I have to go back to school in America."

"You go to university in America?" the man asks. Sylvie nods. "What do you study?"

Sylvie points to the girl. "I want to teach girls her age."

"Not boys?" he asks.

"Both. Girls and boys."

The man places two fingers on Sylvie's shoulder. "Khoda hafez," he says, and then he says something to the girl, who motions Sylvie to follow her back to the street.

At the entrance to the bazaar, the girl takes Sylvie's hand in hers. At first, Sylvie thinks she wants to shake hands to say goodbye, but the girl is turning her hand over.

"For twenty rials I can read your hand," the girl says. Her palms are painted with henna and tattooed with Persian script. The girl studies Sylvie's upturned hand briefly and smiles. "You are lucky," she says.

"What do you mean?"

"These small criss-cross lines below these fingers bring salt luck."

"Salt luck?"

"Yes, salt luck." She rubs the tips of her fingers together. "Only a little bit. A sprinkling. And only sometimes. When you do not expect to be so. And in a way that may not at first seem so."

Sylvie pulls two folded bills from her pocket and flattens them between her fingers. The paper is red and tan. On one side is a portrait of the Shah of Iran; on the other, a lion. Above the lion's head floats a crown. Held high in its paw is a sword.

"Reza Shah Pahlavi," says the girl.

Sylvie looks at her, surprised that she would know. "I prefer the lion," Sylvie says, and hands her the two red notes.

"Two?" the girl asks.

"So you can see both sides."

Walking backwards, the girl waves goodbye with both painted palms. Sylvie waves back waiting for a break in the traffic. Two mopeds pass, and then a boy with a crop, leading a donkey that is wobbling beneath the weight of burlap saddlebags loaded with charcoal. It isn't until she is running that she remembers the girl in her dream. She looks back, but the girl has disappeared with her dog in the crowd.

On the other side of the street, a man squats beside a small smoking fire he has built in the dirt. He breaks twigs and drops them into the flames a few at a time to keep the embers burning. Leaves crack beneath Sylvie's feet as she walks past. Their eyes meet. Sylvie walks faster. She breathes more easily once she has turned the corner onto the street that leads to the hotel. It is a quiet lane. Plane trees shade the sidewalk. A wrought iron fence borders a park. Sylvie glances through the rails as she passes. On the other side two boys are studying on a bench.

One of the boys says to the other, loudly, "You speak English to that girl."

The other boy closes his book and approaches the fence. He looks about Sylvie's age, which is nineteen, though he might be younger. "We wish to practice our English with you," he says. His pencil makes a skipping sound, trailing the iron balusters as he walks her to the gate.

"Why do you want to learn English?" Sylvie asks.

"So I can speak English very well."

They walk a gravel path to the bench where the other boy waits, his chin tucked inside the high neck of his sweater. Sylvie can't tell whether he is shivering from the cold or trembling with nervousness. He is younger. Twelve or thirteen. They look like brothers. The older boy pulls a few rials from his wallet and, pointing to the bicycle that is leaning against the back of the bench, says something in Farsi. The younger boy raises his voice a few notches in protest, but stands. He pushes the bike a little way down the path and looks over his shoulder before he leaps over the saddle and pedals away.

"Beshin," the older boy says to Sylvie.

"Beshin?"

"Yes, *beshin*." He pats the seat. "Sit. *Beshin*." Then adds, "*Mikhahi*. Do you wish?"

"Are you asking me if I want to sit down with you here?"

"Yes. And also, if you wish, to give me some English."

"Okay. For a little while."

"Where have you been?" he asks.

"To the bazaar. With my mother. She wanted to look for Kilim."

"Ah, Kilim. You have been to Bazar-e Vakil. Where will you go now?"

"To the hotel." Sylvie tells him the name of the street.

"I can take you there if you wish," he says.

"But first English."

"Yes. First English."

"I think it would be easier for you to give me some Persian."

"Very well. What word would you like me to give you?"

"What is your name?"

"Hussein," the boys says.

Sylvie laughs. "No. I mean, how do you say, what is your name?"

"Oh. *Esmet chie*."

"Esmet chie." Sylvie enunciates the syllables carefully. She can almost taste them, metallic and ornate in her mouth.

"Esmet chie?" Hussein asks.

"Sylvie."

"Like the metal."

Sylvie smiles. "I was just thinking that Persian tastes like silver."

"Tastes?"

Sylvie points to her tongue. "How do you say, how do you say?"

He laughs. "Chetor migan."

"*Chetor migan* boy?" Sylvie asks.

"Pesar."

Sylvie looks through the tree to the sky. "*Chetor migan* sky?"

"Aseman."

"Moon?"

"Mah."

"*Chetor migan* star?"

"Setarre."

"That sounds like English. I think you're making it up."

"No, no," he protests. "It is true."

"You are funny."

"*Ba-mazzehn,*" the boys says. "*Ba-mazzehn* means funny."

Sylvie smiles.

The boy touches the edge of his little finger to her face. First beside her eye, and then beside her mouth. "Khandidan."

"Khandidan?"

"*Khandidan* means to laugh. Smile and laugh. Both. And did you meet the fortune teller in Bazar-e Vakil?"

"The fortune teller?"

"Yes. In Bazar-e Vakil there is a fortune teller who keeps a small bird. You give the fortune teller so many rials and he directs the bird to pick a bit of paper from a tray on which is written a line or two from Hafiz to guide you. You know who is Hafiz?"

"The poet," Sylvie answers. "No, I didn't meet the fortune teller." She is thinking of the girl with the henna-painted palms. "But I have this." Sylvie reaches inside her pocket and unfolds the slip of graph paper Sahar Jazin gave to her. "The goldsmith wrote it for me." She moves her hair behind her ears. "He made these for me."

Hussein is not interested in the earrings. He studies the small piece of graph paper. "Did the goldsmith tell you what he has written?

"He said it was my name in Persian. Then he wrote something more."

"This is Hafiz. I shall translate for you." Hussein clears his throat. "It is difficult."

> *I beg you, to no one else show / These words*
> *I send in such a hidden way*

Hussein interrupts his translation. "How do you say this word. Something like a secret code. It is a mathematical word. You do not know it?" Hussein makes an impatient noise with his mouth. "In the poem, Hafiz has given the woman he loves a secret code to understand."

"Go on," Sylvie tells him.

> *Read these words in some safe place you find.*

"I don't know how to say the rest," he says.

"Try."

"Only the last two lines":

*You may speak any language to me / Love speaks
every language beneath the sun.*

"That is Hafiz?"

"That is the great Hafiz."

"So I did receive a fortune in Bazar-e Vakil."

"I think so."

"Do you think it is a good fortune?"

"A fortune is not necessarily good or bad."

Sylvie wants to ask him to explain what he means, but the younger boy is back and calling out to them through the rails in the fence. "Do you like ice cream?" He parks the bicycle and unwraps a sheet of newspaper from around several frozen ice cream bars.

"Ice cream in winter?" Sylvie says. It is so cold."

"Yes," he says.

"*Chera?*" Sylvie says. "Why?"

He laughs, pointing to Hussein. "Because of Hussein." Then in Farsi he says, "*Khalikho.*"

"Hassan says your Farsi is very good," Hussein explains.

The younger boy peels the paper from his ice cream bar. "Tomorrow you come back for exam."

"Tomorrow I must go home to Ahvaz," Sylvie says.

Hassan smiles. "Oh. You must go home to your mother-father?"

"My mother is here in Shiraz. At the hotel." Sylvie looks up through the trees. "Tomorrow we must go back to Ahvaz, where my father works. After that, I must go back to school in America."

"Khoda hafez," the younger boys says.

"He tells you, go with God," Hussein says. "Shall I walk with you to the hotel?"

"I know the way. It isn't far."

"But it is almost dark."

"Not dark. Twilight." Sylvie points to the first stars that have appeared in the sky. "*Setarre.*"

"Yes, *setarre.* Later there will be more."

"I will look for them."

"I will also look for them," Hussein says. "I will look for you looking for them. We can meet like invisible lines in geometry."

"And I will look for you."

"Even from America?"

"Even from America."

"Goodbye then," Hussein says. "*Khoda hafez.*"

"When your school will close, you come back to Shiraz," the younger Hassan says. "Goodbye," he says again. "Good everything."

*

It is difficult to remember exactly, but sometimes she tries. That night, unable to sleep, she took the fold of paper to the window and pulled the curtain aside to a night so clear, so black, the stars looked like salt spilled across the sky. *There it will dissolve. This is the Irani way. Salt luck. Only a sprinkling. And only sometimes. In a way that may not at first seem so. A secret code. For you, not for anyone else. We can meet like lines in geometry. Goodbye. Good everything.* And then, when she pressed her face to the glass—she can't be certain—it was so long ago and the night was so dark—it might have been drifting snow, but the way she thinks of it now, the stars were falling. All of the stars of Iran. In a way they've never fallen again.

Yalda & Zhila

I was eleven going on twelve the year my sister convinced my parents to let me spend the summer with her in East San Diego. It was the summer they told us they were getting a divorce. In a letter, my sister told my mother, and my mother told me, that a house full of children lived in a barn in the canyon below her apartment building. She said they had horses. Sometimes when she was in the shower, the letter said, through the window she could hear children singing. She'll like that, the letter said. Let her come. She needs to get out of Ohio.

I spent a few days the first week there, thinking I'd look for them. The apartment was near the end of a dead-end street where the sidewalk ended abruptly at an abandoned construction site. On the other side of a padlocked gate, a steep dirt road led to the barn in the canyon. I saw a tricycle turned upside down on the driveway. I saw a horse trailer and another trailer that looked like it was meant to be a place for someone to live, parked under the eaves of the barn. I don't know if anyone lived on the property or not. I never saw anyone. Maybe they'd moved away. Maybe my sister made it up. But I never saw any horses. And I never heard children singing.

The apartment building was a two-level structure in the shape of an L. At the corner, where the two wings intersected, was a swimming pool surrounded by a chain-link fence. The pool rules were posted on a sign on the wall of the pump house shed. Rule number five was painted in bold red type. "Children under the age of fifteen are permitted to use the pool only between the hours of three and seven pm and only if supervised by a responsible adult."

My sister lived on the second floor. Her front window looked over the parking lot. A girl called Yalda lived with her mother a few doors down. Sometimes I heard them speaking in a language I didn't recognize. I knew her name was Yalda because that's what her mother called out when she couldn't find her. Yalda? Yalda? As if they were playing hide and seek.

Before I knew Yalda, I used to stand at the railing in front of her apartment window because it looked directly over the pool. I had seen a girl about my age standing at the glass watching me through the transparent curtains. At least I liked to think she was watching me, but maybe she was just waiting, as I was, for Mrs. Bigelow, the manager, to unlock the gate to the pool.

When we eventually met, I asked her if she'd ever seen horses in the canyon or heard children singing. She stared at me as if to say, not every question deserves an answer. She could be like that. She was old for her age. She said she was fourteen, but I think she was still thirteen that summer. Thirteen going on fourteen.

I suppose you could say our relationship started to turn into something closer to a friendship when we started whispering together about Mrs. Bigelow's daughter. She was in Yalda's class at school, and she had Tourette Syndrome. Her name was Georgina, but her mother called her Georgie and, because that was the name we heard yelled across the courtyard, we called her Georgie too.

Yalda told me Georgie was a good basketball player. "That's why her knees are knobby. That's why she walks like a boy." Then Yalda would lift her chin and blink her eyes and jerk her head back and forth. Her imitations of Georgie were close, but Georgie's movements weren't limited to her head. Sometimes she shrugged her shoulders and flapped her arms. Sometimes she grunted and hopped on one foot. Sometimes she repeated what one of us had just said. Sometimes she touched us.

One night we were standing at the railing in front of Yalda's window, looking down at the pool. It was after nine. Her mother was out. "A friend of hers is getting a divorce," Yalda said. "She wants to talk to someone who's been through one."

"My parents are getting divorced," I said. "That's why I'm spending the summer with my sister."

Yalda changed the subject. "I'm not sure I believe her, though. I think she might be seeing someone."

I think that was the night she asked me if I wanted to know what her name meant in English. Before I had a chance to say if I did or I didn't, she told me. "It means the longest night of the year."

I stared at her blankly.

"Have you never heard of the winter solstice?"

I shrugged. "I guess I have," I said.

"The winter solstice marks the day of the year with the fewest hours of daylight. I was conceived on the solstice. The twenty-first day of December."

I could tell by the way she looked at me that she was testing me, but, as usual, I didn't understand what the test was.

"The shortest day of the year must have the longest night," she said. Her eyes were impatient. "That's the other reason my parents named me Yalda. Don't you get it?"

I didn't say anything.

"Never mind."

I thought she was tired of me and was going to go inside, but then she told me that Mrs. Bigelow kept a spare key to the locked gate beneath one of the buckets of chlorine crystals behind the pool shed. Georgie had shown her.

We had to stand for a few seconds in the security floodlight that beamed down from the roof. Anyone looking through their sliding glass window could have seen us, but no one came out. I watched the green-lit surface of the pool, rippling in the spotlight, while Yalda pressed the key into the padlock.

It was a smooth fit. Smooth, the way the water was smooth, that seemed warmer at night when I touched it. As we stood in the dark behind the diving board, pulling our t-shirts over our swimsuits, I asked her why her mother called me Zhila. I thought it was her way of pronouncing the G at the front of my name, which was Gillian with a kind of French accent, and what seemed to be an Iranian habit of adding an ah-sound to the end of a word, but Yalda said it was the name of a river.

"A river? That's all?"

"That's all."

"Why would she call me after a river?"

"Because you're so quiet," Yalda said. "My mother said the Zhila is a quiet river. And very slow."

What she really meant, at least what I think she meant, was that I was slow. Maybe they were right.

That night the lower half of my body floated in the deep end of the pool while the back of my head rested on the edge of the deck that felt warm and smooth in the dark and watched while Yalda stood on the diving board and threw the spare key into the deep end. It was a reckless thing to do. She didn't have goggles. If she couldn't find it, we'd be caught. But she always found it, even with her eyes closed. Over and over I watched her dive down to touch the bottom of the pool.

Bubbles rose ahead of her face and her long dark hair lifted and fell like riverweed, brilliantly green in the floodlit water. When she surfaced, she gulped at the air for a breath. I had stroked to the center of the deep end by then. We were facing each other, treading water in the dark, our eyes resting just above the surface. Then, instead of looking away, as I usually did when she looked into my eyes, I looked back, and what I saw in her eyes for the first time was that I might be worthy of her friendship.

She stroked back to the diving board, talking as she swam, as if she had said nothing to insult me. As if being quiet were nothing to be ashamed of. As if it were a quality, in fact, that she admired.

One day towards the end of the summer, Georgie was knocking a basketball against the olive-green wall of the cavern-like entrance to the apartments. The ceiling was arched like a cave and the artificial rock façade of the walls made it feel cool like a cave. At the end of August in East San Diego, the cave-like entrance to the apartments Mrs. Bigelow managed was a good place to stand around. The screen door to Georgie's apartment had a silver frame and was marked with a silver letter B for Bigelow, which made it seem like the cool arched entrance was the doorway to Georgie's personal kingdom.

Yalda was sitting on the curb with the volume turned up on her transistor radio, watching the cars drive by. I was inside the tunnel, leaning against the part of the wall that was covered with rocks, watching Georgie toss the ball. She was very good at catching it on the tips of her fingers when it rebounded. Very good at sending it back without breaking her rhythm. Every once in a while, her neck jerked to the side and her chin shuddered and lifted without control, sometimes for as long as a minute. Then she was herself again, a tall, athletic girl with broad shoulders and strong, brown legs in a sturdy pair of shoes and a loose pair of knee-length shorts, pushing a ball against a wall.

I was used to her Tourette episodes by now. They followed a predictable pattern. First her head would start shaking. Then when that stopped, she would go through a phase where she barked short little phrases that didn't make sense. She usually came out of it in a minute or so. But this time, the barking turned into the mangled words of a song that must have played a thousand times on the radio that summer. Then Georgie was dancing, her shoulders stiff, her arms stretched out in front of her. "Down on Broadway, yeah. There's a dance, yeah." She pulled her arms close to her sides and walked in place. Her knees lifted high like a baton twirler in a marching band. Her hipbone cocked one way and then the other. "Funky Broadway. Funky, funky Broadway." When she couldn't think of any more of the words, she stopped and stared. Her face was sweaty, and a little bit of saliva had gathered at the corners of her mouth.

Yalda was beside me by then, watching Georgie dance. Listening to Georgie sing. To anyone watching we would have looked like partners in meanness. But we weren't. We'd never been partners. Then Yalda was pointing her finger. I hadn't even noticed. A stream of urine was trickling down the inside of Georgie's smooth, brown, basketball-strong legs, puddling on the concrete between her shoes.

"Only an imbecile pees on the ground in broad daylight," Yalda said. For a split second her eyes held mine with what I wanted to believe was the conspiratorial smile she shared only with me. Then her face cracked open with laughter and she was yelling for me to run.

I hadn't wanted to, but I had nothing else to do, so I followed her back to her apartment. I didn't run, though. She was already inside when I reached the door. I watched her through the kitchen window, leaning over the plates and glasses stacked at the bottom of the sink, splashing her face and the back of her neck, gulping the water that was cupped in her hands. She was supposed to wash the dishes before her mother came home from work. She was supposed to keep the front door locked. But Yalda didn't much do what she was supposed to do. That was the day she showed me the quail eggs. And that was the day the way I felt about Yalda changed.

"Shall I introduce you to the members of the family we left behind?"

I followed Yalda into the living room where she stood in front of what she called the étagère, the stack of shelves that held what was left of the mementos her mother had brought from Iran. She pronounced the word étagère the French way, which she had already told me several times she spoke fluently, and pointed to the faces in the ivory framed photographs, positioned like a shrine on the lowest shelf. "This is my mother as a girl. These are my mother's sisters. And these, I suppose are my cousins. To think we might have been friends. The tall man standing behind the chair is my grandfather. My mother's father. We lived with him for a time in Shiraz. The man in the chair wearing the white turban is my grandfather's father. My great-grandfather."

"What about your father? Don't you have pictures of him?"

"My father? If there were any photographs of my father, my mother would have burned them. I haven't seen my father since we left Iran. He was a petrochemical engineer. When I was three or four, he took a job with an American oil company in Ahvaz, a city in the southwest province of Khuzestan. My mother didn't want to live in Ahvaz. She considered Khuzestan too rural, too poor, so she and I moved into my grandfather's house in Shiraz, which was where we lived until my father wrote to say he had been offered a job teaching at an institute of technology in California. He said he would go ahead of us. He said he would send for us when he was established, which he did. I guess he changed his mind. He was supposed to meet us at the airport in Los Angeles when we arrived, but he sent someone else in his stead. I was eight. Eight going on nine by then. My mother forbids me to speak of him. So I don't."

I wanted to open the small painted boxes on the shelf above the photographs. "What about these?"

"These," Yalda said, "are made of papier-mâché." This word she also pronounced the French way. The boxes were black and just the right size to hold in my hand. One was slightly longer than the other. The lid of the larger one was painted with red-faced flowers and yellow birds with yellow beaks and long, yellow tail feathers. I was already thinking of the things I could hide inside the box if it were mine. The surface of the smaller box was painted with people dressed in orange robes, gathered in a garden.

"You can recognize the difference between the men and the women by their headgear," Yalda said. "The women wear chadors. The men wear turbans. In the old days, the turbans came in all different shapes and sizes. Some were decorated with long trailing tassels and adorned with jewels and peacock feathers or ostrich feathers. Others were embroidered with yellow finches like the ones on these boxes and small quail with crested head plumes."

There are coins in this one," she said, opening it for me to glimpse inside before she snapped the lid closed again.

"What's inside the box with the yellow birds?"

Yalda looked as if she couldn't remember and pried the lid open to check. "Only a piece of paper."

I could see handwriting scrawled in pencil across a narrow sheet of graph paper. "What does it say?"

"Sahar Jazin. It's someone's name. Gold and silversmith," she translated. She closed the lid to change the subject. "We didn't always live like this," she said, looking over her shoulder at the Formica table pushed under the kitchen window, the dishes stacked in the sink.

Then, out of nowhere, as if the memory of a dream had just then crossed her mind, she said, "My grandfather hid quail eggs in his turban."

"Your grandfather wore a turban?"

"Of course. Didn't you notice his turban in the photograph?"
She pulled the photograph of the family portrait from the
shelf for me to see again. "He always wore a black turban. He
was a very devout Muslim. My mother told me that when my
grandfather was a boy in the 1920s, Reza Shah Pahlavi, who was
then the shah of Iran, banned the turban because he considered it
unmodern. But many men, such as my grandfather were defiant
and refused to accept the decree. My mother said he wrote a
letter to the shah and signed it with the words of the Prophet
Muhammad: "My community shall not fall away so long as they
wear the turban." Finally, those who could prove that they wore
the turban as a symbol of dignity and piety were allowed to carry
on the tradition. Perhaps my grandfather foresaw that the man
my mother married would one day take us away from Iran. I
think he wanted me to understand what was important to him
before we went away."

"What do you think he wanted you to understand?" I asked.

Yalda glared at my density. So I asked another question. "Why
did he hide quail eggs in his turban?"

"It was a game. Quail eggs are very small." Yalda held her
thumb and forefinger apart. "Four or five of them could fit easily
inside this pencil case. I'll show you." Yalda pulled a barstool
from the kitchen in front of the étagère and climbed on top of
it. Resting on the highest shelf, a bird's nest was pushed away
from the edge out of sight. She lifted it down carefully and set it
on the chest in front of the couch. It was an ordinary bird's nest
made of twigs and dried grass. Maybe because of its shape or
maybe because the grass was wound around and around on itself,
it reminded me of the turbans she had described. Inside, six quail
eggs rested like six spotted stones. Each was different from the
next. Some were pure white and some were a pale brown-white.
Some of the spots were points, like freckles; others looked like
splotches of spilled ink.

"The shells are empty now," she said, "otherwise we wouldn't
have been able to save them. They're very old and very fragile. I'm
not supposed to touch them.

"When we lived in my grandfather's house in Shiraz he made a great ceremony of coming home at the end of the day. I remember him entering the house wearing a heavy wool coat that reached past his knees. I always thought of his coat as the robe an emperor would wear in a fairy tale. I was always so happy to see him.

"My grandmother had died years before, and my mother worked in an office, so an old woman looked after me during the day. But she was very stern. She couldn't read, and she didn't like to play games, so I spent my time in my imagination or I looked out the window or at pictures in books. When my grandfather walked through the door, I would run to him and wrap my arms around his knees. He was very tall. I remember thinking of the dark space under his coat as a kind of fortress, and there I would hide until he coaxed me out to play the game."

"How did you play it?"

"It was something like hide and seek. I was to turn my back and cover my eyes while he went into the kitchen to hide the quail eggs he had brought home from the market in the folds of his turban. Then I had to search for them with my hands. But I had to be very careful so they wouldn't break when my fingers bumped into the shells. My mother says my grandfather invented the game because I was slow to speak. Quail eggs, it was believed at the time, would help children who were late talkers to express themselves. But it wasn't that. I remember very well. It wasn't that I couldn't speak. I didn't have a speech impediment. I just didn't want to talk."

"I'm that way," I said. "I mean, I can be. My sister says being too quiet makes a person look dumb. She said people who are unable to speak are called dumb."

"Mute," Yalda said, and then, as was often the case, she turned the conversation back to herself. "The game had rules. Each egg I pulled out of his turban I had to assign a word. *What kind of a word?* I asked him with my eyes. *Anything you like,* his eyes said back. *Look around the room. Open your book.* And so I pointed, and he would say the word, and I would repeat it, and the sound that came out of my mouth rose like a shape in the air."

"What would you do with the eggs after you found them?"

"The old woman who looked after me pricked the ends of the shells with a needle and blew the contents into a dish. Then I had to eat them. My grandfather said it was the only way the words would stick.

"We put the last eggs that I pulled out of his turban inside this nest. It used to sit on a shelf in his house. Now here it is in this apartment in East San Diego."

Sometimes when Yalda's mother was out late, and late for Yalda's mother sometimes meant all night, I spent the night with her. We closed the curtains and locked the front door and slept together in her mother's wide, double bed. But we never went to sleep right away. Yalda liked to talk to me about her life in Shiraz before she moved to California. But only in the dark. Maybe her memory was clearer in the dark. Whatever it was, she told me things in the dark that she wouldn't have ordinarily revealed about herself. I don't think she realized that it gave me a kind of advantage.

"In my grandfather's house there was a small door in the living room wall that opened onto a kind of cellar," she told me one night. "It wasn't an ordinary cellar. It was the cistern, where the household water was stored."

"Didn't you have indoor plumbing?"

"Oh, yes. There were pipes under the floors that carried the water to the kitchen and the bathroom and the washing machine in the laundry room. But the water didn't come from the city or from a well in the ground. It came from the cistern."

"How did the water get inside the cistern?"

"The rain. We drank rain water. I washed my hair in rain water. Sometimes in the dry season, a water truck came. A man dragged a wide canvas hose across the living room floor and, when he turned a switch, all of the water in the tank on the back of the truck emptied into the cistern.

"The door in the wall was the size of a tea tray, the size of a small window shutter. It was made of wood and you turned a small metal latch to open it. If you leaned your head inside, you could see that the cistern was the size of a room. A cold, dark room. The water didn't fill the room, and you couldn't see to the bottom, but sometimes you could hear a sound. Like water lapping against the limestone wall.

"I didn't like to open the door in the wall. I used to imagine a drowned girl in a white dress lying half-submerged at the bottom of a well. I could even see a ribbon floating with her long black hair in the rain water. I think I thought she was me. Or what was going to become of me."

I didn't tell Yalda, but when she described the girl's hair floating in the water, I saw her hair, green as river weed, lifting and falling in the floodlight the way it had looked the time we went night swimming.

"Sometimes I thought I heard another sound. I thought it was the drowned girl's head knocking against the limestone wall."

"Did you tell anyone about the girl in the cistern?"

"Not until now," she said. Then she took my hand in hers and held it between her ear and the pillow until she fell asleep.

The clock on the radio beside her mother's bed was illuminated. Blue numbers on an orange face. I watched the minute hand circle the clock until it was after two in the morning. I needed to use the bathroom. Then I wanted a drink of water. I filled a glass at the kitchen sink and took a sip. I dried my hands on the tea towel hanging on the oven door and looked from the barstool pushed under the counter to the swath of light the security floodlights projected onto the living room wall.

I watched my shadow move across the wall as I carried the barstool toward the shelf of mementos. What I really wanted to take was the papier-mâché box painted with the yellow birds, but there were only three boxes. A box would be too easy to miss. I stood on the stool and reached for the nest on the highest shelf. Did anyone really know there were exactly six eggs inside of it? If weeks or months from now, after I'd returned to Cincinnati, when

Yalda or her mother looked in the nest, would they even notice one was missing? I didn't think they would. I reached cautiously into the nest and remembered how the winding layers of grass and string and twigs had seemed like the turbans Yalda had described, and I imagined Yalda's three-year-old fingers, reaching inside the folds of her grandfather's turban until they bumped against one of the quail eggs.

My touch was not so delicate. The first shell crushed into papery shards. I used only the tips of my fingers to lift the second egg out of the nest.

I remembered seeing an extra-large bottle of aspirin in the medicine cabinet and carried the quail egg, balanced on the palm of my hand into the bathroom. I closed the door and listened for Yalda before I turned on the light. The cap came off easily and, as I'd guessed, there was a thick wad of cotton pressed down on the tablets inside. The quail egg, resting on a sheet of Kleenex beside the sink, looked like a small potato, speckled with a constellation of black stars. I pulled the cotton apart and made a nest for the egg between the layers. My overnight bag was unzipped on the floor where I'd left it. I hid the aspirin bottle inside and slipped back into bed beside Yalda.

*

Sometimes at night I hold Yalda's quail egg in my mouth and wait in the dark to see if it has given me the courage yet to say what I think. Sometimes while I'm waiting, in my mind, I write Yalda a letter. It always ends the same way. *Maybe I just wanted to say to you what you said to me so many times with your eyes. You shouldn't have trusted me. And you know what else? You were right. Not every question deserves an answer.*

Alice in Abqaiq

Twice a day, just before dawn and just after dusk, Saturday to Wednesday in compliance with Saudi Arabia's work week, the Aramco bus travelled sixty kilometers through the desert between the small, gated community of Abqaiq and Dhahran, the oil industry's administrative center for the Eastern Province.

The route was elliptical and began in the dark beneath a streetlight in front of the Abqaiq commissary. Once on the highway, the night sky turned red-lit and hazy. The flames from the natural gas burn off rose hundreds of feet in the air and reflected off the sand for hundreds of miles. There was always the smell of sulphur in the air.

The bus was a modern, air-conditioned Mercedes Benz, dark green with a white roof. The windows were clean and the seats were comfortable, but there was little to see. Blowing sand. Blowing dust. The raised hood of a broken-down truck on the side of the highway. The smashed front ends of the unlucky cars that had suffered head on collisions, left in the sand to be gutted for parts. Some mornings, as the flare-lit sky faded to a grey haze, a caravan of nomads could be seen in the distance, directing their camels along invisible tracks to the Rub' al-Khali, the largest sand desert in the world. The expatriates called it the Empty Quarter.

At 6:30 a.m., the bus made a rest stop at the commissary in Dhahran. An hour later, it carried the Dhahran passengers and those, like Alice, who had boarded in Abqaiq, on to the city of Al-Khobar, situated, she had been told, though she hadn't seen for herself, somewhat picturesquely on the western coast of the Persian Gulf. If teachers or staff members signaled the driver, the bus made a brief stop outside the gate of the international school before travelling on to the city center of Al-Khobar and the King Fahd International Airport before it circled back to Dhahran. The bus repeated the journey three times in each direction with rest stops in between, and then returned to Abqaiq at the end of the day.

Alice substituted occasionally at the international school. Her father worked for the Arabian American Oil Company as a petrochemical engineer. After she had graduated from college with a teaching credential, she travelled to Saudi Arabia to visit her parents, thinking she would find work at one of the company schools and save some money before she decided what she would do next, but Aramco had an obscure regulation barring dependents of employees from working full time in the Kingdom unless hired from their home country. There was a loophole, Alice learned soon enough. She could work temporarily as a substitute at the international school.

Riding the bus through the desert was something to do, but the work was unsatisfying. Sometimes when she was called in, instead of taking the Aramco bus to the school, she would spend the morning walking the tree-lined streets of the Dhahran compound, looking at the sprinklers turning on the manicured lawns of what could have been a suburban neighborhood in Texas or Arizona. It was like playing hooky.

Sometimes she stashed her swimsuit in her school bag and spent the morning at the Dhahran pool, which was larger than the pool in Abqaiq. Sometimes she went to the library and thought about what it was going to take for her to finally leave the security of the idle life she had started to lead in Saudi Arabia.

Sometimes she sat in the commissary, drinking coffee and forgot about the time, reading a book. Sometimes she sat in the commissary, drinking coffee and surveyed the men. There were thousands of engineers and geologists and accountants and contractors and offshore oil rig hands, who should have been, she thought, at her disposal, though few took the initiative to speak with her. Perhaps they presumed she was looking for a husband, while they were in the Kingdom for the short term. For the money.

On other mornings, if Alice had worn long sleeves and remembered to pack the shawl she had found in her mother's bottom drawer in her school bag, she took the bus all the way to Al-Khobar and wandered through the Old Souk, where the streets were rubble, and the roofs were flat on the two-story cinderblock buildings. Saudi men in ankle-length thobes and head scarves that draped over their shoulders stood at the doors of their shops, propped open on rusty hooks like shutters, or sat on a street corner, smoking and talking and rubbing their beads. Indian or Pakistani women walked by in pairs wearing saris the color of flowers and birds. The Saudi women walked always in groups and dressed always in long, black abayas and long black head scarves called niqab with only a slit for the eyes.

In the 1970s, as it was, the abaya and the hijab were not yet compulsory for foreign women, but the Mutawwa, the religious police, were said to travel in public watching for violations. She had heard the stories. A teenage boy tied to a post and lashed with a whip for stealing fruit. A bucket of paint thrown at the bare legs of a foreign woman wearing a knee-length skirt. A woman from the freer, though still Muslim island nation of Bahrain, stoned to death in the public square for committing adultery.

For her sojourns to the Old Souk, Alice pulled the shawl from her school bag that was long enough to cover her head and wrap around her shoulders. Dressed this way in her make-shift hijab, she felt free to walk down King Khalid Street, where she tried on jewelry in the gold shops and stopped at a coffee bar for a tiny glass of espresso sprinkled with cardamom and served with dates. Sometimes she found her way to Prince Bandar Street, called Al-Suwaikit by the local merchants, where she touched the metallic threads woven into the hijabs and the coins and sequins sewn to the abayas and caftans in the clothing shops. Once a store clerk had almost persuaded her to try one on, but when she noticed him eyeing the curtain that only partially covered the opening to the dressing room, she held the caftan in front of her and told him she could see it would fit without trying it on. He wrapped it in brown paper and tied it with string.

In the afternoon, Alice returned to the Al-Khobar city center and waited for the Aramco bus that would take her back to Dhahran. If there was time, she stopped in the commissary for a Coke. Then, at six p.m., she took the last bus of the day back to Abqaiq.

There were two drivers. One was an older Saudi man who wore
a white skull cap instead of the more commonly seen red-checked
head scarf. He kept his eyes on the road in front of him as he
drove. He didn't much like to talk. The other driver was young
and dark. He might have been twenty-eight; he might have been
thirty-two. Maybe it was because the gold-rimmed, aviator style
sunglasses he wore made him seem almost cosmopolitan. Maybe
it was the way his head nodded from side to side and the way he
smiled when he greeted the passengers as they signed the manifest
beside his seat, but Alice found him handsome. Once, the young
driver asked her as she boarded the bus to go home if she had ever
visited the beach in Al-Khobar and mentioned, when she told him
she hadn't, that he sometimes took his afternoon break there at the
end of the seafront road. There were no services, only a parking lot,
but the offshore breeze was cool.

*

Sometimes, like today, whether absentmindedly or intentionally,
Alice missed the bus that would drop her on the side of the
highway outside the gate of the international school in time to
walk the paved road to the office before classes began.

Behind the commissary, in the shade of the rainbow shower
trees that lined nearly all of the streets of the Dhahran compound,
was a taxi kiosk, a cinderblock bungalow with a red tile roof, and a
heavy screen door. Alice was reasonably sure that the man behind
the counter knew who she was; it wasn't the first time she had
missed the bus, but before the door had even banged shut behind
her, he turned his back on the long wooden counter that separated
his office from the waiting room.

Alice studied the fringed ends of his ghoutrah, the red-checked
head scarf that hung down the back of his long white thobe.
She watched the slowly turning blades of the ceiling fan for a
few moments, and then finally said in halting Arabic, "*Aedhirni.
Excuse me. I have missed the bus to Al-Khobar. Will you call a
taxi for me please?"

The taxi man took his time sipping from a small glass of tea before he turned around. "Lays 'aya taksi," he said civilly enough. But when he explained in English that no taxis would be available for many hours, that he couldn't tell her when one would return, his voice sounded faintly curt. She could wait for the next Aramco bus in the cafeteria at the commissary. He touched the thick, double black cord, clamped like a crown to the top of his head that held his headscarf in place. Or, if she preferred, he motioned to the row of straight-backed wooden chairs situated against the wall at the back of the room, she could wait here. He could offer her a glass of tea.

He must know she had just come from the commissary, but Alice was careful to maintain both the distance and the decorum he had used with her. "Shukraan," she said, thanking him in Arabic. Then in English, "I will go to the pool." She then asked the taxi man if she might use his telephone. She should let the secretary at the international school know that she wouldn't be coming in today.

*

The Dhahran pool was located a few blocks from the taxi kiosk within the walled courtyard of the community center, a modern complex that contained outdoor tennis courts, indoor racquetball courts, a bowling alley, a snack bar, the pool, and the library. Since the day ahead was long and the temperature was beginning to rise, Alice went first to the library, which was air-conditioned, to read the want ads in the *International Herald Tribune*. This week a teaching position was advertised at an international school in Rabat. An English writer living in Auvillar needed an assistant. A couple sailing the Greek islands for an extended period needed a tutor for their children. In her mind she wrote a letter to the writer in France, detailing her skills and talents. Then she went to the dressing room behind the pool where she changed into her bikini. The bikini was green. Dark green like the bus, though she hadn't thought of that until now, studying herself in the full-length mirror on the wall. Dark green with a pale blue racing stripe along the edge. She took a company towel from the shelf and walked to the far end of the patio where a few tables were arranged in the shade. There was only one other person on the premises, and that was Hassan the attendant, who was on his hands and knees at the other end of the pool picking leaves off the surface of the water with his fingers. She watched to see if he would look at her when she shook the towel over one of the longue chairs, but he didn't lift his head.

Agitated, she dived into the water without goggles or a cap and swam the length of the pool hard and fast. When she paused to catch her breath once, Hassan was folding towels in the shade of the attendant's stand. He didn't appear to be in the least aware of her. She pushed off the edge of the deck, gliding underwater for a few yards, then pulled herself forward, kicking hard, length after length, until she was out of breath and her eyes burned from the chlorine.

*

At a quarter of three, Alice opened the screen door of the taxi kiosk, which the taxi man kept dark because the room seemed cooler that way. It was true. Her hair was still wet and her bare arms in the sleeveless polo dress she had worn that day, smelled faintly of coconut oil. She was early, but instead of waiting in the cafeteria at the commissary, she had decided to see if she could coax the taxi man into having a conversation with her.

He greeted her politely enough. In fact, his voice seemed livelier than it had earlier that morning, but he was preoccupied at his desk with receipts and an adding machine. Alice took a seat in one of the chairs at the back of the room and watched the leaves of the trees shaking in the wind through the screen door. She was rearranging the contents of her school bag and had just started to leaf through a folder of student papers, when the taxi man lifted the section of the counter that served as the entrance to his office.

"See here," the taxi man said rather excitedly. "Sudip is here." He held the screen door open on its hinge, and the young bus driver who had brought Alice from Abqaiq at 5:30 that morning walked into the room. "Sudip takes tea with me before he makes the journey back to Abqaiq for the night," the taxi man said, pouring the bus driver a glass of tea from the jar that he kept on his desk. "He practices his Arabic with me. I practice my English with him."

The bus driver wore tight-fitting trousers made of a shiny fabric and a long-sleeved paisley-patterned shirt tucked neatly inside a narrow belt. He apparently hadn't noticed that Alice was seated at the back of the room because, when the taxi man asked her from behind the counter if she would like another glass of tea, addressing her in Arabic as *anisatan*, young miss, the bus driver turned sharply.

Alice hadn't known his name was Sudip. She had been riding the Aramco bus from Abqaiq to Dhahran and on to Al-Khobar for several weeks now, and she was always glad when she saw that he, rather than the older Saudi man, who was stern and didn't seem to like to speak to women, was the driver. Sudip seemed aware of this. Lately, if the bus wasn't full, he had begun to motion for Alice to sit in the row behind his seat and, through the wide rearview mirror, he spoke freely with her on the hour-long ride through the desert. On one of these occasions he had informed her that he was not Saudi, but from Kolkata, a city that was much more modern, much more progressive than Al-Khobar. When he smiled at her, it was as if to say, he too was from somewhere else, as if to confirm that they shared a kind of secret, and perhaps they did.

Today in the taxi kiosk he didn't smile at Alice. Today his fingers trailed self-consciously through his black hair, which he wore longish and oiled back behind his ears. Today, even though the room inside the taxi kiosk was dark, he pushed his gold-rimmed, aviator-style sunglasses firmly against his face and glanced at the watch on his wrist as if he were going somewhere.

"I will make one more journey to Al-Khobar," he said. Alice

wasn't sure if he was speaking to her or to the taxi man. "I will take my break on the seafront road." Then he faced Alice directly. "Have you not yet visited Half Moon Beach?"

When the taxi man saw that Alice was considering Sudip's half-suggested invitation, his face darkened.

He looked from the dark glasses that covered Sudip's eyes to Alice's bare legs. His voice was quiet, his tone severe. "The social customs foreign women keep on the grounds of the Dhahran compound do not prevail beyond the gate." His eyes scanned Alice from shoulder to wrist as if he were skinning her arm with the blade of a knife. "If you go to Al-Khobar dressed as you are, you must not disembark the bus."

Sudip waved to the guard as he drove through the gate and the turn signal clicked as he merged into the traffic on the newly surfaced highway. Alice sat behind the driver's seat and watched Sudip's face concentrating on the traffic through the rearview mirror. As she suspected, the bus was empty. They drove past the gate of the international school and then past the turnoff that led to the University of Petroleum and Minerals.

"Why is the taxi man so stern with me?"

Sudip laughed. "It is not you. He is this way with every woman. Non-transactional communication between the sexes in public is forbidden."

"What do you mean?"

"If not for the purpose of business, communication between the sexes is to be avoided. Yusef would prefer to avoid communicating with foreign women altogether, but his taxi business is operated by the Aramco transportation department. In this case, his communication with you must be laced with an unwelcome undertone. To honor Saudi tradition."

"His name is Yusef? I didn't know that. I never knew your name until today."

"But I know yours. Your name is Alice. I have known your name for many weeks."

Alice looked away from the rearview mirror and directed her attention to the view outside the window.

Even though Alice had made the conscious decision to ride the bus alone with Sudip; even though the taxi man had heard Sudip mention the name of the beach; even though the bus was a registered company vehicle; when, she watched Sudip bypass the familiar roundabout, where he normally would have turned had he been making a scheduled trip to the Al-Khobar city center, a small feeling of alarm began slowly to grow inside her chest. Then Sudip was turning the bus onto the highway that led to the coast, a way she had never been before.

Alice watched the road signs. King Khaled Bin Abdul Aziz Street turned into King Fahad Bin Abdul Aziz Road. By the time the bus bore right onto a road called the Custodian of the Two Holy Mosques Road, the last of the buildings on the outskirts of Al-Khobar had disappeared. They turned left onto Al-Khadiyah Road. The roads grew rougher, the farther they drove.

At first the desert was a barren series of rolling dunes, but as they drew closer to the gulf, the round sand hills became stiff-edged cliffs, layered with mineral lines of dark green and blue. Clumps of brush grew low to the ground. From the top of a crest Alice saw a scattering of squat-looking palm trees, and then a dark flash of wind-blown water.

Sudip turned onto the narrow, sand-coated seafront road and brought the bus to a stop in front of a jetty made of piled boulders and blocks of concrete. Long streaks of foam blew off the white caps and floated on the surface of the brown-green water.

"Here you have Half Moon Beach. Named after the half-moon shape of the road," he added. Sudip opened the door with the lever beside the steering wheel and ducked his head to walk down the steps.

Alice smelled brine in the air but remained in her seat and looked at the gulf through the window. They were parked in an empty parking lot. There were no other vehicles. No restaurants. No shops. No street vendors. No one.

Sudip leaned his head through the open door. "Come outside, Alice" he urged. "You must breathe the sea air."

Alice felt uncomfortable hearing him use her name. He had become too familiar too fast. "I can smell the gulf from here."

Sudip mounted the steps slowly. Alice pulled her school bag close and touched the railing on the partition that separated her seat from the driver's seat in front of her. She pulled on the hem of her dress. Her bare knees felt exposed. Sudip wrapped his hand around the cool silver rail and, for a moment, their hands rested side by side. Alice could feel the heat of his skin.

"We should go back now," she said.

Sudip looked at his watch. "We have time still. Come. We can walk beside the water. You will like it."

"No. The bus is scheduled to return to Abqaiq soon. We need to go back now."

*

At six o'clock, the bus pulled away from the curb in front of the Dhahran commissary for the last return to Abqaiq. All of the seats were filled. Engineers who lived with their families in Abqaiq but worked in an office in Dhahran. Saudi businessmen who worked in Al-Khobar, but lived in the less crowded, less expensive apartment buildings located behind the wall of the Abqaiq compound. Women from the Philippines or India or Pakistan, who worked in Abqaiq as domestic help returning home from a day of shopping.

Two women dressed in bright saris sat across the aisle from Alice. One was the bright green color of the skin of a lime. The other, a deep red-brown, woven with gold thread. The younger woman wore gold bangles on her bare arms and what appeared to be a diamond stud in one of her nostrils. The other woman, who was slightly older, wore large, dangling gold earrings and many gold necklaces. Her forehead was marked with a round spot of rouge. The women turned often to glance at Alice then laughed into their hands and spoke to one another in Hindi. Alice hadn't realized she had been staring.

Their eyes darted from Sudip's reflection in the rearview mirror to Alice. The slightly older woman's gaze travelled the length of Alice's bare arm and rested on her fingers, bare of rings. She looked from Alice's knees to the leather sandals that were the same color as the tanned skin of her feet. Sudip smiled behind his dark glasses at the women. Soon he had joined their conversation. Alice could not understand them. She heard a questioning tone in the women's voices. The word "American" mixed into the wash of Hindi that came from Sudip's mouth. The women repeated the word, accenting the "i" in the middle of the word with a kind of gasp, as if they were astonished that a young American woman would be travelling by bus unaccompanied.

Alice noticed the same sense of loneliness she felt at the commissary when the expatriate men did not return the attention she paid them. The same agitation she had felt at the pool when Hassan had refused to look at her lying on the longue chair in her bikini. She would have liked to talk to the women. She would have liked to know what the red mark between the woman's eyebrows signified and what it was called.

Just then Sudip stopped talking and glanced at Alice as if he had felt her question. She looked away, imagining that they had been talking unfavorably about her. Then she decided to be bold. She tapped the center of her forehead with the tip of her finger, shrugged her shoulders, and raised her eyebrows. "What do you call this?" she asked the older woman, who had talked the most and was watching her the most closely. English was spoken in India, after all. Wasn't it?

Through the rearview mirror Sudip spoke to the two women in Hindi and nodded the side of his head in Alice's direction. The women laughed openly.

"Bindi," the older woman, who was sitting closest to Alice said. Then she seemed to be instructing Sudip to translate for her. She spoke in Hindi. Sudip spoke in English.

"Every morning, after a Hindu woman takes a bath," Sudip said to Alice, "she must sit in prayer."

The woman raised her voice impatiently as if she wanted Sudip to be more thorough.

"Of course, one cannot sit in prayer the whole day," Sudip continued. "So when the woman leaves the prayer room, she is expected to put some mark on her forehead to remind her throughout the day about all of the activities she has done and has yet to do."

The woman interrupted him.

"Also," Sudip added, "the bindi is to remind you of the purpose of your life. It is obvious you cannot see the mark on your own forehead every time, so whenever you see it on another face you will get a chance to remember all of the things you are in the middle of doing and all of the things you have yet to do."

"What is it made of?" Alice asked. "How do they put it on? How do they form such a perfect dot?"

Sudip must not have known the answer to this because he said something more to the women, who explained.

"It is a powder. A kind of powder that can turn to paint."

The women were very interested in Alice now. They tilted their heads and raised their chins at Sudip's reflection and raised their voices too.

Alice felt herself growing uncomfortable again. She didn't know how much Sudip might be telling them about her. About his relationship with her. Though the existence of a relationship between them had not been expressed. And then Alice began to wonder if the women were also attracted to Sudip. If perhaps their conversation with him was a form of flirtation, safe in the public presence of the other bus passengers.

"Does the bindi mean a woman is married?" Alice asked.

Sudip nodded. Alice looked from the slightly older woman's forehead to the younger woman wearing the sparkling stud in her nose. Perhaps she was the woman's daughter. Perhaps she was her sister. Perhaps the older woman had it in mind to make a match between Sudip and her daughter or her sister. Alice wondered where they lived. Because they didn't live on the compound. Abqaiq was a small community. She would have noticed women wearing saris if they had ever walked the streets of Abqaiq. Then she wondered where Sudip lived in relation to the women. And what they did while he was working. And what they did when he was home.

*

In the days and weeks that followed the three-way exchange that had taken place between Alice and Sudip and the two Indian women, Sudip's behavior changed. And she did think of it as a three-way exchange, not four, because the younger woman wearing the diamond stud in her nose and the sari that was the color of the skin of a lime, not the dark green of the bus, had only watched. Now when Alice boarded the bus, Sudip sometimes greeted her with a smile, but it was a polite, formal smile, as if it were meant more for the benefit of the other passengers than for her, especially when he addressed her in Arabic as Yousef had in the taxi kiosk with the word *anisatan*, young miss, then kept his gaze aimed at the road for the hour-long drive to Dhahran.

Sometimes she caught his reflection looking at her for long moments through his gold-rimmed, dark glasses, and then, as soon as their gaze met, he directed his attention back to the road ahead. It was as if he were playing a game. She had thought that she knew him to some extent, and that he knew her. And yet he seemed to want to pretend that he did not. At the same time, he seemed to want for her to see and to feel the scant but weighty attention he sometimes cast in her direction like a handful of salt. Like a spell. She recognized some of his mannerisms and found herself looking for them. Waiting for them.

Halfway through the journey to Dhahran, for instance, he had a habit of pulling a white cloth from his shirt pocket and using it to clean the dust from his sunglasses. Then, after folding it back into a neat white square and sliding it back into his pocket, he used his thumb and middle finger to push the sunglasses firmly against his face. If the day was warm, he rolled back the cuffs of his sleeves and shook the gold watch that gleamed on his wrist. Sometimes when he found her looking back at his reflection in the rearview mirror, his fingers twisted the steering wheel anxiously and his leg trembled beneath his shiny, silver trousers and he spoke quietly under his breath as if he were praying. Alice was not religious to speak of. She had never considered that Sudip might be. She had never considered the differences between a Hindu man and a Muslim man. He had seemed so modern.

*

Then came the morning he spoke to her directly once again. It was a day in December. The days were colder now. Alice wore jeans and a sweater. She wore socks and a pair of desert boots she had bought in the Old Souk. She wore a knitted cap. When she boarded the bus in the Abqaiq darkness, Sudip smiled at her in the old way, as if to settle once and for all that they shared a secret.

"Will you go to school today, or will you walk the streets?"

It was a funny sounding option, as if some days she played the part of a prim school mistress and other days took on the role of a streetwalker.

"Today I will go to work," Alice said, and pushed her school bag across the empty row of seats behind him.

Alice stared through the window at the flare-lit sky in the distance and waited for the pale red disc of the sun to rise on the horizon. Twenty minutes or so into the journey, Sudip and Alice began to talk through the wide rearview mirror that looked silver in the early morning, winter light. Their conversation was casual. Light. Easy. Not quite hungry. Still, she could not ignore the distinct tickle of appetite between them.

*

Alice hadn't given Sudip her parents' telephone number. She supposed it would have been easy enough to look up. Everyone was required, after all, to sign the manifest each time they boarded and disembarked the Aramco bus. In any case, he had begun to call the house. At first, if her mother answered the phone, he hung up. If she answered, she pulled the extension cord out from under the rug and took the phone into her bedroom, where they talked in the evening dusk or sometimes, if he called later, in the dark. In the beginning he was sweet and polite. It was like being a schoolgirl again, lying on the floor with her legs outstretched and her feet on the wall, like a sloth, her father called her telephone talking position. In the beginning, Sudip asked simple questions. What book had her students studied in class? What had she eaten for dinner? Soon his questions turned bolder. What was she wearing right now? What did she wear when she slept? Did she find herself opening her eyes unexpectedly in the dark? Did she think of him in the night? He thought of her. And in the dark, when he thought of her thinking of him, he imagined what her skin felt like beneath the white t-shirt she had told him she slept in. Until finally he couldn't stop himself from asking her to meet him.

Tomorrow or, if tomorrow was too soon, the next day. Or the following day. He could wait. He would ring. They would simply arrange where he would park the bus, and then she could meet him there. He had an hour after the last return from Dhahran before he was to return the bus to the transportation warehouse. It would still be dusk. Not dark. Still light. She would be safe with him.

"There is an empty lot not far from your father's townhouse. A construction site for the new subdivision. The workmen will be gone by then."

Alice sat up, startled. "How do you know where I live?"

"Your father picked you up at the Abqaiq commissary when you disembarked the bus one day. He drove a red truck."

"There are lots of red trucks on the compound."

"Only one has his registration number. I circled every street of Abqaiq until I found it. I recognized the flat roof upstairs. It was just as you said. I saw the glass door that leads to the room where you sleep. The white curtain moved. I will drive that way each day at seven o'clock. Then I will drive to the empty lot and wait for you. It is no more than a ten-minute walk. I will wait for you to come."

"I can't meet you in an empty lot. What if someone sees us?"

"The bus can be our disguise."

Alice wore a long, brown caftan embroidered with gold thread. The sleeves were also long. The collar opened in the shape of a V on her chest, but there were long gold tassels to tie it closed at the neck. She stood in front of her mirror and studied the shape of her breasts through the lightweight cotton. It was 1977. Alice didn't wear a bra except to work. Too provocative, she decided and pulled the caftan back over her head. She searched her top drawer for the black tank suit she never wore to the pool and pulled it over her hips. The fabric was thick and elastic. The straps snapped against her shoulders. It was tight. She slipped the caftan back on and slid her hands down the front of her body. The tank suit flattened her breasts and held her body firm. She left the house through the sliding glass door in the kitchen.

"Where are you going?" her mother called from the living room.

"To watch the sunset. I won't be long."

The bus was parked on the side of the road in the unfinished subdivision at the back of the compound. Only the blacktop roads were installed. Only the concrete curbs. Only the lines of the lots, marked with bright small flags on spikes hammered into the hardpacked desert sand.

The door of the bus was open. Alice stood at the foot of the stairs and looked at Sudip sitting in the driver's seat. He stood when she reached the top of the stairs. He had removed his dark glasses. She glanced at them on the dashboard. Without them he seemed older. His eyes looked tired. He took her elbow in his hand and coaxed her down the aisle. Not all the way to the back of the bus, but farther back than she had sat before. He chose a row of seats on the right side of the bus, out of view of the rearview mirror.

It felt strange to be on this side of the bus. It was almost as if the rearview mirror had been a protector of their public selves. A chaperone. Now they were alone. Being alone with him now felt different from the time they had been alone at the end of the seafront road that faced Half Moon Beach. Or maybe it felt exactly the same. She didn't know what she was doing. She didn't know what she wanted. And then she did. She didn't want anything anymore. It was a taste in the mouth. A certainty.

Now he was reaching for her. He touched her face and pulled her close to his chest. She could smell his skin. His ears were too close to her face. She turned away. She was glad when he reached to touch her that, because of the tank suit beneath her caftan, it wasn't her skin that he touched.

He backed off when she pushed him away. "What do you want?" Alice asked.

"I only want to be alone with you."

"Do you think you will marry me? Do you think my father will arrange for you to move to the United States? Is that what you want?"

"I only want to be alone with you. I only want to smell your skin."

"You live in a room in a boarding house behind the Abqaiq Souk. You will never be for me. I can never be for you."

Sudip said nothing.

"I guess it is fortunate that men are not required to wear the mark of the bindi," Alice said. "Otherwise you would have to remember all of the things you have done and all of the things you are in the middle of doing and all of the things you have yet to do."

*

Alice stopped answering the telephone. She stopped accepting substitute assignments at the international school. She stopped riding the bus to Dhahran. She spent her days in her parents' townhouse, leafing through the atlas and studying old *National Geographics* in search of a plan. She had found Paul Theroux's *The Great Railway Bazaar* in the Abqaiq library and had thought she might fly to Istanbul and take the legendary Orient Express to Paris, but when she wrote a letter to the rail company, requesting route information, the response said the line had made its last journey in May of that year.

Sudip did not give up easily. This time when her mother answered the telephone, he asked to speak to Alice. When her mother told the caller that Alice wasn't home and asked who was calling, he persisted. Until finally, Alice's mother told her that she was never to speak to this man again. He was never to phone the house again.

How could she tell him not to call if she couldn't speak to him?

Surely Alice understood the consequences of her actions. This isn't California, you are living in the Kingdom of Saudi Arabia. Had she not read about the Dutch woman who had been arrested and detained in Qatar on suspicion of adultery?

Alice hadn't, but understood now that her mother had found and read the journal she kept in her chest of drawers with the box of matches and the pack of Marlboros she sometimes smoked.

Like every surface exposed to the Abqaiq sky, the flat roof outside of Alice's bedroom was coated with a fine, white layer of sand. The stars were sharp behind the gauzy red haze of the flare-lit sky, and the middle-of-the-night air felt almost cool. She rested her chin on the palm of her hand and smoked part of a cigarette and drew patterns with a matchstick in the fine layer of dust on the ground until first light when, even in winter, the flies came. But before she dragged her bedding inside and fell back to sleep in her cool, white sheets, a black formation of birds blew across the sky in the shape of a sphere. She wondered if Sudip could see them too, driving his bus across the desert from Abqaiq to Dhahran, as he must be right now, and what Yusef the taxi man might tell him a sighting of black birds moving in unison like that in the direction of the Empty Quarter might portend as they drank their glasses of tea in the kiosk behind the commissary until it was time to drive the bus to Al-Khobar.